THE
First Third
WISH

THE
First Third
WISH

Ian Beck

Barrington Stoke

First published in 2013 in Great Britain by
Barrington Stoke Ltd
18 Walker Street, Edinburgh, EH3 7LP

www.barringtonstoke.co.uk

Text © 2013 Ian Beck
Illustrations © Ian Beck

The moral right of the author has been asserted in
accordance with the Copyright, Designs and
Patents Act 1988

ISBN: 978-1-78112-245-7

Printed in China by Leo

This book has dyslexia friendly features

For my grandson, Sebastian Beck

Contents

Chapter 1
Cobweb Messes Up

Once upon a time there was a young fairy who was very new to the job. Her name was Cobweb. For Cobweb's first task, Miss Dandelion, the head fairy, sent her to take three wishes to a kind old wood-cutter.

Cobweb flew off on her new wings
and posted the first wish into the
wood-cutter's letter box.

The next day she posted the second
wish down his chimney.

On the third day something terrible happened to the third and final wish.

On the way to the wood-cutter's house, Cobweb somehow lost the shiny little wish.

Cobweb panicked and flew back along the paths to look for the wish. But there was no sign of it anywhere. Poor Cobweb knew that she would be in terrible trouble when she got back to Miss Dandelion's office.

Cobweb also knew that the poor wood-cutter was waiting for his third wish. So she opened her magic pack and broke out the spare wish that all fairies carried in case of emergencies. She delivered the wish by leaving it for the wood-cutter to find in his seven league boot.

Chapter 2
Dickon Sets Off

That same morning a nice young man called Dickon Barleycorn set off on the high road. He had all he owned in the world tied in a bundle on his back. He even had his little telescope, for he loved nothing more than looking up at the

stars in the night sky. He was a tall and handsome fellow, but he had no money and he was a bit of a dreamer. He was off to seek his way in the world.

'Who knows,' Dickon thought. 'If I am lucky, I might make my fortune. And if I am really lucky, I might find a damsel to rescue and marry. If not, then I will just enjoy the adventure.'

It was a warm summer's day. "A perfect day for adventures," Dickon said out loud as he set off.

After a long morning of walking, Dickon was tired. He sat down to rest on the stump of a tree and ate some bread and sausage. He was thirsty now too.

"I'll have to look round for a nice cold stream in a minute," he said.

Then Dickon spotted something bright and shiny among the leaves on the ground. It was hard to say what it was, but he liked the look of it and so he picked it up. It shone in his hand like one of the stars in the night sky.

"What a funny-looking little thing," he said to himself. "But it's pretty. I reckon I'll keep it!" He stood and stretched his arms wide. "I wish I had a nice cold bottle of lemonade right now," he said.

Dickon took a step forward and his boot clinked against something. There at his feet was a dark brown bottle with the stopper still in it. He picked it up. It was icy-cold to the touch. There was a label which said –

Home-made Lemonade

"Well, there's a bit of luck," he said. "Just the thing I wanted."

He broke the seal, opened the bottle
and tasted the drink.

"Best lemonade I ever tasted," Dickon said. He drank it all and then put the empty bottle into his bag. He felt much better.

Chapter 3
Cobweb Gets in Trouble

By this time Fairy Cobweb had flown back and told Miss Dandelion what had happened.

"You lost the third wish?" Miss Dandelion cried.

"Yes," said Cobweb. "Sorry!"

Miss Dandelion's wings began to flap in panic. "This is awful, Fairy Cobweb!" she said. "It means that there is a whole wish out there on the loose."

"I know," said Cobweb. She hung her head in shame.

"A wild wish! A lost wish! Why, anyone could pick it up and wish for anything at all!" said Miss Dandelion. She shook her head. "A lost wish has no limits," she said. "The person who finds it could make as many wishes as they want."

"More than three?" poor Fairy Cobweb asked in shock.

"Any number of wishes!" said Miss Dandelion. "Why, they could wish away us fairies and all other wishes if they wanted to! Fairy Cobweb, you'll have to go and get that first third wish back before it's too late."

Chapter 4
Dickon Meets an Old Lady

———

Dickon marched on all afternoon.

The first person he met on the road was an old lady. She was calling out in distress as she walked. "Kitty? Here, Kitty! Here, Kitty, Kitty!" she called.

"Have you lost something, ma'am?" Dickon asked.

"Oh, indeed I have, young man," the old lady said. "I let my cat out and now I fear she has run away. I've been looking for such a long time, but there's no sign of her."

"I could help you look," Dickon said. He took off his hat and bowed. "Dickon Barleycorn at your service! Now, what kind of a cat is she?"

"She's a tabby cat and her name is Kitty," the old lady said.

"Why, I wish I could snap my fingers and make your old Kitty walk out from those trees there," Dickon said. He snapped his fingers with a click.

"Well, would you believe it?" the old lady said. "Look! There she is, the cheeky old puss."

And, sure enough, a tabby cat walked out from the trees by the road.

"Well, well," said Dickon. "It looks like you are in luck, ma'am."

"Better than luck," the old lady said. "I can't thank you enough for what you did, young man. I shall have to keep Kitty on a lead in future!"

"I did nothing at all, ma'am," Dickon said.

"But you did," said the old lady. "You have a gift. Use it well."

"If you say so, ma'am," Dickon said. He was puzzled as he set off again. After a while he began to puzzle some more. Where would he spend the night?

"I wish I could turn the next corner and find a nice snug inn," he said to himself.

He turned the next bend in the road and there was a snug old building. It was an inn – the only one he had seen all day. It had a sign outside which read –

The
Traveller's
Rest

The inn looked warm and welcoming. Dickon could smell good cooking too. It all looked just right.

"Well, there's another bit of good luck," Dickon said to himself.

After supper, Dickon went to his room in the inn and looked out of the window at the summer stars.

After that he fell into bed and slept like a log.

Chapter 5
Two Young Ladies Out at Night

———

While Dickon slept in the cosy inn, two other people were not sleeping at all.

At one end of the kingdom, poor Fairy Cobweb was out alone in the dark. She was searching for any clues as to where the missing wish might have got to.

In the forest, Cobweb found traces
of a traveller who had walked among
the trees. First, she spotted part of a
sausage sandwich. Then, a little further
on, she found the stopper from a bottle
of lemonade. She knew the lemonade
had been wished for as there were
traces of fairy sparkle dust on it.

Cobweb went further along the road
and met an old lady with a cat on a lead.
The cat also had traces of fairy sparkle
dust on its fur.

Cobweb appeared in front of the old lady at human size. "Good evening," she said.

"Oh my! A fairy!" the old lady said. "I half expected you. I knew that boy had the gift."

"Which boy?" Cobweb asked.

"The boy with the wishing gift," the old lady said. "His name was Dickon Barleycorn and he used a wish to find my lost cat, Kitty."

"Do you know where this boy went?" Cobweb asked.

"He walked down the road that way," the old lady said. "Do I get a wish then, my dear?"

"I think you've already had one," said Fairy Cobweb. She pointed to the cat. It still sparkled.

At the other end of the kingdom, a princess named Isabella was running away from a man she did not love and did not want to marry.

First, Isabella threw everything she loved best over the high castle wall. There was not much. The thing she loved best was her own little telescope, which she used to gaze at the stars. She put that in her pocket. Then she climbed down the wall on a rope she had made of all her silk bed sheets tied together.

Isabella was soon dashing along the road that snaked into the forest, away from the castle.

Chapter 6
Star-gazing

Dickon was woken in the middle of the night by a great fuss at the door of the inn. He peeped out and saw the inn keeper let in a pretty young woman who looked out of breath and worried.

"Need any help at all?" Dickon asked from his door. He half hoped she would say yes.

"No, thank you," the girl said.

Dickon thought she seemed very proud as she spoke. "I wish I hadn't said anything to her now," he said to himself as he clicked his door shut.

A second later he heard the same fuss start up again. When he looked out, the inn keeper was letting in the same girl with the same pretty face and the same long dark curly hair. All the same, all over again.

'I must be dreaming,' Dickon thought. This time he said nothing to her at all, and went straight back to bed. But he couldn't sleep and so, after an hour or so, he got out of bed and fetched his telescope. He opened his window and looked out at the night sky.

"Ooh," he said out loud. "It's so clear tonight! Look! There's Perseus and Andromeda."

"Who said that?" the dark-haired girl called from the next window along.

"I did, Miss! Dickon Barleycorn's the name. I was just looking at the stars."

"So was I," the girl replied.

"It's a good night to see them," Dickon said.

"It's perfect," she replied.

"But I like the winter sky better," Dickon told her. "Then you can see Orion."

"Oh yes! So do I," said the girl. "I thought I was the only one."

"So did I," said Dickon.

"Not any more!" the girl said.

"No, so it seems. Well, goodnight, Miss," Dickon called.

"Goodnight, Dickon Barleycorn," the girl replied.

While they were talking at their windows, Fairy Cobweb flitted in through the keyhole in Dickon's door. She had seen that the inn also sparkled, and so she knew Dickon had wished for it as well.

Fairy Cobweb rummaged through Dickon's bag and pockets and there she found the sparkly missing wish.

Cobweb pulled the wish out and tucked it back in her fairy pack where it would be safe and could never be used again.

Before he went to sleep, Dickon said to himself, "I wish I could meet and marry a girl who loves the stars just like the one I met tonight."

Chapter 7
The Search

___

In the morning the alarm was raised far away at the castle. Princess Isabella's room was empty. Princess Isabella was missing!

The King had never liked the man that his ministers wanted Princess Isabella to marry. It was all for the good of the kingdom, because the kingdom was poor, and the man was old but rich.

The King didn't say it, but he was pleased that Isabella had the spirit to run away.

"She can't have gone far," one minister said. "Her horse is still here."

"Well, I suppose we should go and find her and bring her back," the King said.

"It's a little late for that," another minister said. "The rich man has left in a very bad temper. He'll never marry the princess now. Our money chests are empty. We needed his money! What shall we do now, Your Majesty?"

"Make a wish?" the King said with a sigh.

"I don't think wishes will help," the first minister said. "Look! Even the Royal Purse is empty."

The King and his ministers set out to find the princess. After a long morning of riding, they came to the Traveller's Rest.

"I don't remember this inn being here before," the King said. "Let's ask for the princess in case she's here."

"Yes," said the inn keeper. "There was a young lady with dark curly hair here last night. She arrived all in a flurry."

"Well, where is she now?" the King asked.

"Why, she is out in the garden," said the inn keeper. "She is talking about the stars to that nice young Mr Barleycorn, who also arrived yesterday."

The King and his ministers found Princess Isabella and Dickon sitting beside a sun dial. Princess Isabella stood up and introduced the King to Dickon.

"Oh, I beg your pardon, Your Majesty," Dickon said. He bowed low. "I had no idea that Miss Isabella was a princess."

"Father," Isabella said. "I wish to marry Mr Barleycorn. He loves the stars and the planets as much as I do. He is the perfect match for me."

"Pardon me, Sire," the chief minister said to the King, "but this young man does not seem rich. In fact, he looks very poor. Stars and planets are all very well, but the kingdom needs some gold ..." His voice trailed off.

"I wish your coffers and your purses could all be full of gold all the time," Dickon said. "But even if they are not full ever again, Isabella and I will still marry and live happily ever after."

"That's right," said Princess Isabella. She drew herself up to her full height and looked her father in the eye.

The chief minister felt a sudden heavy weight in the Royal Purse that he wore on his belt. He peered inside and saw that it was stuffed full of shining gold coins. He looked up.

"Perhaps it would not be such a bad idea after all for these two to marry," he said.

"What's changed your tune?" the King asked.

"Oh, I don't know, Your Majesty," the chief minister said. "Young love written in the stars, perhaps."

And so they all set off together back to the castle where the wedding would be held. The ministers were over the moon to find that the Royal Coffers were just as full of gold as the Royal Purse.

Chapter 8
Cobweb Finishes the Job

Fairy Cobweb returned to Miss Dandelion
and handed over the shining thing she
had found in Dickon's bundle.

"Here it is," she said.

Miss Dandelion looked down at it. "What's this?" she asked.

"The missing first third wish," said Cobweb.

"Look at it!" Miss Dandelion said. "Look at it properly and what do you see? I'll tell you what I see, shall I? A lemonade bottle top covered all over in fairy wish sparkles. That's what I see!"

"Oh dear," said Cobweb.

"I'm afraid your job isn't finished yet," Miss Dandelion said. "Back you go and find that missing first third wish before anything else goes wrong."

After a happy wedding and a wonderful honeymoon, Dickon and Princess Isabella were out in the garden one night looking up at the sky.

"I wish we had an observatory and a proper telescope all of our own," Dickon said. "Then we could look at the night sky in winter and stay warm."

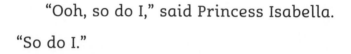

"Ooh, so do I," said Princess Isabella. "So do I."

As if by magic, a sparkling new little observatory appeared in the castle gardens that night.

Not long after that, poor Fairy Cobweb flew to the castle and looked through Dickon's old clothes and belongings again. There at last she found the shiny little first third wish in a deep pocket of his old trousers. She flew back across the forest and handed the wish to Miss Dandelion.

"Well done, Cobweb," Miss Dandelion said. "Good work. But please remember to be more careful with your wishes in the future."

"I will," Fairy Cobweb said.

Later that year Dickon and Princess Isabella both discovered new stars in the night sky. Dickon named his star Isabella and Isabella named her star Dickon. Of course, they both lived happily ever after.

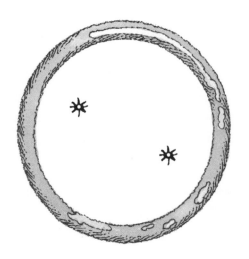

Our books are tested
for children and young people by
children and young people.

Thanks to everyone who consulted on
a manuscript for their time and effort in
helping us to make our books better
for our readers.